Drive Me Wild

Jessica Coulter Smith

Printed in the United State of America

ALL RIGHTS RESERVED.

No part of this book may be reproduced, stored in a retrieval system, or transmitted, in any form or by any means, without the prior permission in writing of the publisher, nor be otherwise circulated in any form of binding or cover other than that in which it is published and without a similar condition including this condition being imposed on the subsequent purchaser.

Publisher's Note:
This is a work of fiction. All characters, places, businesses, and incidents are from the author's imagination. Any resemblance to actual places, people, or events is purely coincidental. Any trademarks mentioned herein are not authorized by the trademark owners and do not in any way mean the work is sponsored by or associated with the trademark owners. Any trademarks used are specifically in a descriptive capacity. Font used in this novel is Garamond.

Cover created by Jessica Coulter Smith
FIRST EDITION
ISBN 978-1-482-32453-2
©2012, Jessica Coulter Smith

Other Books by Jessica Coulter Smith

Whispering Lake
Magnolia Magick
Eternally Mine
Yuletide Spirit
Night's Embrace

Luna Werewolves series
Vicus Luna (book 1)

Books in the Ashton Grove Series
Moonlight Protector (Book 1)
Moonlight Hero (Book 2)
Moonlight Guardian (Book 3)
Moonlight Champion (Book 4)
Moonlight Savior (Book 5)

Vaaden Captives
Sorcha
Enid
Susan

Vaaden Warriors
Rheul
Randar
Thale

Short Stories
For Now and Always
Creole Nights
Love at First Bite

Chapter One

His kiss was like liquid fire, scorching her very soul. The taste of him drove her wild. Her heart was pounding in her chest, loud enough that she was sure he could hear it, hard enough that he had to feel it. Skin to skin, yet not close enough. She wanted him and she wanted him *now*. He'd teased and tormented her for the last half hour with soft caresses, heated looks, naughty comments whispered in her ear. Enough was enough!

She reached between their bodies, her hand firmly grasping his large cock. The feel of velvet over steel made her even wetter. She didn't think it was possible for him to get any harder, but then she hadn't thought she could get any wetter and now she was dripping down her thighs. She rubbed her legs together trying to ease the ache that had been steadily growing.

With a wicked smile, she kissed her way down his body until she knelt before him. His cock jutted from a dark nest of hair, proud and strong, practically begging for her attention. She leaned forward and licked the bead of precum from the head of his cock, drawing a groan from the commanding man standing above her. Knowing that she could literally bring him to his knees if she so desired made her feel powerful.

She licked his cock from base to tip loving the salty-sweet taste of him. Slowly, she took him in her mouth, easing her lips down the steely length of him until she'd managed to swallow him whole. She pulled back, gently gliding her tongue over him. Fingers tangled in her hair, urging her on, wanting her to go faster. She thought about teasing him, drawing it out longer, making him pay for the torment he'd put her through, but decided to take pity on him. Men were such fragile creatures after all.

Sucking and licking his cock in earnest, taking him in until he bumped against the back of her throat, over and over again, she thrilled over every moan and whispered word of encouragement that slipped between his lips. And just as she had him on edge, ready to topple over, she stopped.

"What the fuck? I was right there!"

She grinned. "I know, but I have plans for you."

He narrowed his eyes and lifted her to her feet, backing her toward the sofa. With firm hands, he grasped her waist and flipped her around so that she faced the back of it. He used his body to urge her onto the plush piece of furniture, putting her on her knees, open and ready for him.

She gripped the back of the sofa, waiting. He placed his hands on her hips and without notice plunged his cock inside of her hungry wet pussy. She gasped and threw her head back, biting her lip to hold back a moan. She'd never felt anything so wonderful in her life. She'd had large cocks before, but none as big as his. It filled her, stretched her, made her want to beg for more.

Gripping her waist in a vise like grip, he began thrusting with long, hard, powerful strokes, each one deeper than the last. Her nipples peaked and her body hummed. He began to move faster, triggering the biggest orgasm she'd ever had. A kaleidoscope of colors burst behind her eyelids and she pushed back against him, never wanting the sensation to end.

Just as she was coming down from her high, she felt him slide deep one last time and come inside of her. Briefly, she cursed herself for being so careless as to forget a condom, but what was done was done. She'd had her Depo-Provera shot a month ago so she didn't have to worry about getting pregnant. She only had to hope that he was the kind of man who usually didn't forget a condom and was therefore clean. She was usually protected so she knew she wasn't carrying anything.

She felt him ease from her body and she collapsed against the sofa cushions. Never had she felt so satisfied, nor had she ever wanted to keep a man before. But she knew this one wasn't one who played for keeps. He'd made that clear when she'd picked him up in the bar. Not to mention she'd seen him around, a different woman every night. What else could she expect from a guy who rode a Harley like he was part of it?

"I wasn't too rough, was I?" he asked, sitting down and pulling her into his arms.

She grinned. "No, you were just right."

"Considering that we just fucked each other, maybe it's time we swapped names."

"Why? So you'll know what to call me when you're bragging to your buddies about getting laid tonight?"

He chuckled. "I don't brag."

"Bailey Sanders."

"It's nice to meet you, Bailey. I'm Alex Mendos."

"Now that we've been properly introduced, think we can do that again?" she asked.

"As much as I would love to, I have to be at work early tomorrow. But," he said as he reached for his pants and withdrew a business card from his wallet, "I definitely wouldn't mind a repeat performance sometime."

"I thought you didn't do more than one night stands."

"I'm willing to make an exception."

She smiled. "Then I just may call you."

He leaned in and kissed her, a meeting of lips and tongues. When he pulled away, he began to dress. She watched from her position on the sofa until he was finished, then she walked him to the door. After one more mind melting kiss, she told him goodbye and locked the door behind him.

She sighed and made her way into the bedroom. After laying out her nightgown and a pair of panties, she walked into the bathroom and started the shower. It took the water a minute to warm up, but once it was good and hot she stepped under the spray and closed her eyes in bliss. She smiled as she thought of her brief but wonderful encounter with Alex. He'd said he wouldn't mind seeing her again, and she definitely wouldn't mind a repeat performance. Maybe she'd give him a call in a week or two.

She got out of the shower and dried off before getting dressed for bed. Her bed should look inviting since it was after midnight, but she found that she wasn't tired yet. Regardless, she pulled back the covers and slipped between the sheets. She reached over to her nightstand and picked up the book she kept there. This time it was an erotic romance featuring a Navy SEAL. She'd always loved a man in uniform and had had her share of them.

Barely able to concentrate on her book, it wasn't long before her eyes started to droop shut. She closed the book and turned out the light. While she didn't have to start work at any particular time, she set her alarm for nine o'clock to make sure she didn't oversleep and rolled over and closed her eyes. In minutes, she was asleep.

* * *

Alex glanced over his shoulder at the closed door and smiled. He hadn't lied when he'd said he'd like a repeat performance. If it didn't go against everything he believed in, he would've been mighty tempted to stay the night. Assuming she'd have let him. Making love to her all night long was appealing.

There was something about Bailey that spoke to him. The moment he'd laid eyes on her he'd known he had to have her. She was sexy as hell, and when she'd smiled at him, all he could think about were her lips wrapped around his cock. And she hadn't disappointed in that area. Hell, she hadn't disappointed him in any area. The woman was like a stick of dynamite.

He got on his Harley and headed for home. Any other night, he might've gone back out, but not tonight. Not after Bailey. Something told him his life was about to change. Being in Bailey's arms had been beyond incredible. There were no words to describe how he was feeling. It should've scared him, but he faced it with a calm acceptance.

While he didn't know Bailey very well, he had a feeling she was going to be someone important in his life. If she called. He was so used to women chasing after him, begging for his number, that he wasn't used to actually *wanting* one to call.

Alex pulled into the garage at home and killed the engine on his bike. He closed the garage door and went inside. It was nights like this that his home felt so empty. If Bailey did call, perhaps he'd invite her over. It would be the first time a woman, other than friends, had stepped foot in his house. That thought should've shocked him, that he was willing to open himself, and his home, up to a woman he just met. But she wasn't just any woman. She was Bailey.

Everything hinged on Bailey.

Chapter Two

Days later she could still feel Alex's lips against hers, feel his long, hard cock inside of her pussy. Instant lust slammed through her just thinking about him. She had his card sitting on her coffee table and she'd been tempted more than once to call, but she didn't want to seem desperate. No, she'd decided that if she were going to call him, and it was looking likely, then she would wait at least a week, maybe longer. Longer might be better.

She'd used her trusty vibrator every night, but it hadn't been enough. The thought of sleeping with just anyone didn't hold any real appeal to her. She wanted Alex. She wasn't sure what it was about him that drove her wild, but she found that she craved him. She'd thought of little else since he'd walked out her door.

Pushing away from her desk, she went to refill her coffee cup. Her creativity just wasn't flowing today, which was a bad thing. She had several projects due by tomorrow and she hadn't done much of anything on any of them. One way or another, she had to focus. Who would have thought that staring at naked male torsos and couples in erotic positions could be so difficult? She'd always enjoyed her work. Designing book covers, bookmarks, and an occasional magazine cover was fun for her. Except now all it did was make her think about Alex 24-7.

Shaking her head, she sat back down and scrolled through the model images she had to work with for the first project. It was a ménage romance cover and seeing the couples with two men and one woman made her shiver in delight. She'd only tried a ménage once, right after high school, but now that she had more experience she wouldn't mind trying one again. She wondered if Alex was one who liked to share.

Growling, she slammed her hand down on her desk. She *had* to get the man out of her mind dammit! He might be good looking and more than wonderful in bed, but she couldn't waste her time thinking about him. He'd told her before she'd brought him home that he was a one night stand kind of guy. So what if he said he wouldn't mind seeing her again? Just because he wanted to fuck her again didn't mean he wanted a relationship with her, and after their brief time together, she knew that's what she wanted from him -- stability. She wanted to know she was the only woman in his life.

A good, solid relationship sounded good. It had been years since she'd been in one, and maybe it was time to find someone special again. Of course, she didn't think Alex was the right person for the job, no matter how much she might wish otherwise. She needed to turn away from the one night stand offers and look for someone more stable. She glanced at the models on her screen again. Or maybe some*ones*.

Having a new purpose, she decided that tonight would be club night. She didn't usually go out except for Friday and Saturday nights, but there was no reason she couldn't have fun on a Wednesday. It was doubtful the club would be half as full, but surely she could find some men to dance with, and maybe someone worth talking to.

Focusing on her project again, she got back to work. The sooner she finished, the sooner she could get ready to go.

***

A skintight black dress hugged her curves, stopping mere inches below her ass. Matching strappy sandals adorned her small feet. With her purple streaked hair pulled back and a simple choker around her neck, she looked like sex personified. She knew that dressed as she was there was a good chance she would only attract the attention of men looking for a good time, but she could hope that others would look her way, too.

The music in the club was booming and people cluttered the dance floor. She made her way to the bar and climbed onto one of the vacant stools. Ordering an Irish coffee, she settled in and observed the crowd. There were more women than men, but that didn't deter her. Even if she didn't find what she was looking for tonight, she could still have fun.

Bailey sipped her drink as her eyes scanned the men in the room. In the corner, she saw a group of men cutting up and having a good time. She was surprised to see that Alex was among them. Part of her wanted to go over and ask him to dance, but she refrained. While she wanted to have another taste, it wouldn't help her long-term plan much. She tore her gaze away and looked around again. Her view was suddenly blocked by a deep blue button down shirt.

Looking up, she smiled in surprise. It wasn't just one man standing in front of her, but two. Identical twins at that. Mm-mm. The night was looking up.

"May I help you gentleman?" she asked.

"We were hoping you might like to dance."

"With both of you?" she asked, her gaze taking in their tousled black hair and bright blue eyes. In that regard, they reminded her of Alex. They were tall like him too, but not as well built. Not that they were tiny by any means, their muscles just weren't as... well, Alex's muscles had muscles. It was hardly fair to compare anyone to him.

The first one nodded. "I'm Andrew and this is my brother Adam."

"I'm Bailey, and I'd love to dance."

She sat her drink down and followed them onto the dance floor. Sandwiched between them, she let the beat carry her. One of her favorite songs was playing and she just let go. Dancing with wild abandon, she felt their hands caress her. She smiled and ground her hips against the one in front of her.

He placed his hands on either side of her and pulled her closer, his brother moved in even closer behind. She could feel their heat surrounding her. And then suddenly, it was gone.

She blinked and realized that someone had taken her arm and jerked her out from between the hot twins. Looking up, she saw Alex glowering down at her. What was his problem?

"Are you quite done?" he asked.

"No, actually, I'm not. If you don't mind, I'm dancing."

"Is that what you call it?"

She tilted her chin up. "It's what *you* called it last weekend."

Alex motioned for the twins to take a hike, then pulled her off the dance floor into a quiet corner of the room. He released her and she rubbed her arm.

"What's wrong with you?" she demanded. "I was having fun!"

"I told you to call me."

"What you said was that it had been fun and you wouldn't mind doing it again sometime. That doesn't translate into me not dancing with other men."

"I didn't like seeing you with them."

"You're not the kind of guy I need right now, Alex. You don't want to be tied down, and I'm not going to tie myself to a guy who can't commit to me." She turned and walked off a few steps before facing him again. "Don't interfere again."

She heard Alex curse behind her as she walked back toward the bar, intent on downing another drink. Instead, halfway there, she changed her mind and left the club. She heard footsteps behind her but didn't think anything of it. It wasn't until the sound was directly behind her that she got a little nervous. Glancing over her shoulder, she stopped in the middle of the sidewalk.

"What are you doing?" she demanded.

"Making sure you get to your car okay."

"Alex… what do you want from me?"

He shrugged. "A chance to get to know you would be nice."

"But you don't do relationships."

"Who said we had to call it a relationship?"

"Well, that's what I'm looking for. And if you aren't capable of that, then turn around and walk back inside and find you a quick ride for the night, because it won't be me. What do you do, anyway, come down here every night looking to get laid?"

"One of the guys got engaged this morning. We came out to celebrate. I haven't been here since Saturday night."

She bit her lip. "Me neither."

"Look, at least let me walk you to your car."

"I walked."

His eyebrows rose. "You walked?" His gaze raked her from head to toe. "In that?"

"I didn't want to be bothered with parking down here. It's only a few blocks to my apartment."

"Then I'll drive you home."

"Alex…"

He pulled her into his arms and she melted against him. No matter how much she wanted to fight him, she just couldn't resist him. Having his arms around her felt wonderful, and she remembered what it had been like to have his naked flesh pressed against hers, to have his cock inside of her. Breathing him in, she practically purred.

"Let me take you home," he whispered in her ear.

She nodded and let him walk her to his car. He opened the passenger door and she slid into the beautiful black Mustang. The car was sleek and powerful, just like its owner. The interior smelled like him and she inhaled deeply before he got in.

The drive to her apartment was silent. If he had anything on his mind, he was saving it for when they got upstairs. Upstairs. Now there was a thought. He was going to be in her home again. They'd never made it to the bedroom last time, would he expect to get there this time? Was that why he wanted to take her home? Did he just want a repeat performance? Not that she really minded. She had been craving him since the moment she'd laid eyes on him, and the craving just got worse and worse. Even now her mouth watered at the mere thought of sucking that long, hard cock of his.

He parked and helped her out of the car. They walked up the stairs to the third floor and she let them in to her apartment. His business card still sat on her coffee table, a brilliant white rectangle against the dark wood. Alex walked over and picked it up.

"Were you ever going to use this?"

"It's only been a few days."

He dropped it back onto the table. "I had hoped you would have called by now. I've been thinking about you."

"You have?"

"Every second of every day." He moved closer, pulling her body tight against his. "Remembering the taste of your lips, the scent of your soft skin, the feel of your pussy as it gripped my cock… Thoughts of you have been driving me mad."

He'd thought of her? He hadn't just forgotten her once he'd walked out of her door? She smiled and leaned her head against his chest. Her hands rested on his upper arms, strong arms, arms made for holding and protecting. *Thud. Thud.* His heart pounded and she wondered if he was just immensely turned on right then, or if he was nervous. She knew he wanted her, she'd seen the bulge in his pants before she'd gotten in his car with him. Hers was pounding too, mostly from desire. She wanted him, more than she'd ever wanted anyone before. Only Alex made her feel this way. Why? What was it about him that called to her so? She'd been attracted to men before, but with Alex there felt like there was something more.

"I've thought about you, too," she admitted softly.

He leaned down and gently captured her lips with his. She trembled in his arms and leaned into him. His tongue slid into her mouth. He tasted of whiskey and pure male lust, and she couldn't get enough of him. Bailey felt her pussy grow wet and she wondered if he could smell her desire. She'd skipped wearing panties tonight so she wouldn't have a panty line with her dress. Had he noticed?

Alex caressed her thighs and slowly slid her dress up to her waist answering her question. It seemed there would be no foreplay tonight. His hands caressed her bared flesh, making her shiver. He backed her to the wall and she unfastened his pants.

She shoved them down to free his cock and grasped him with her hand, needing to feel him.

He urged her legs around his waist and placed his cock against her wet slit, and with infinite tenderness, he eased inside of her. He stretched her and filled her until she knew she couldn't take any more. Alex was the absolute perfect size for her. Using slow, long strokes, he drove her to distraction. She clawed at his shoulders and back. Everything in her body tightened and strained, reaching, grasping, and then she was tumbling over the edge into her first orgasm.

He began thrusting into her faster and harder and one orgasm turned into two, and just as the second one was ending, a third one began. She screamed out his name as he came deep inside of her.

Alex lowered her to the floor and pulled her dress over her head, dropping it to the soft carpet below. He unfastened her bra and cupped her breasts in his large, rough hands. Her nipples hardened against his palms and she moaned. Already she wanted him again. Would she ever get enough?

"Why don't you go take a shower?" he said, kissing her softly. "I bet the hot water would feel good about now."

"Are you going to join me?"

"If I do that, I won't leave and I think it's best if I head home."

She nodded, having expected his answer, and followed him to the door.

"I want to see you again," he told her. "Promise me you'll call this time? Or do I need to get your number so *I* can call *you*?"

"I'll call."

He grinned and stepped out into the hall, closing the door behind him. "Lock up," he called through the wood door.

She put the chain in place and clicked the deadbolt home. Leaning her head against the door, she listened as he walked away. Yes, she would call him, but she hadn't said when. The man was dangerous. He made her want things that she doubted he could give her. He was amazing in the sack, but that was probably all they had between them. She'd wait and call him when she had an itch to scratch again, and then she'd see what happened. If the man ever stayed the night, or hung around after fucking her, then she'd have hope that something more could come of the odd relationship.

***

Alex drummed his fingers on the steering wheel. He hadn't meant for things to go quite that far, not that he was sorry. Being with Bailey was amazing, no matter how short the time might've been. If possible, this time was even more remarkable than the last.

He'd seen the look on her face when he'd declined her offer to stay. Disappointment. But he'd known if he stayed, he wouldn't have left until morning. And while the idea intrigued him, he wasn't sure it was the best idea. He'd only stayed the night a few times in his life, and the others hadn't gone well. But oh how he would love to wake up with her wrapped in his arms!

Now that he'd seen her again and told her to call him once more, maybe he'd hear from her. When he'd seen her sandwiched between those two guys at the club, he'd almost lost it. As it was, he'd still acted a bit of a caveman, dragging her off the dance floor. But she'd left him little choice. He found it hard to believe she hadn't seen him in the club. He was certain she had looked him over and dismissed him in favor of the two admittedly good looking guys she'd been dancing with.

All right, so he'd noticed her the moment she'd walked in to the club. He could've asked her to join him, but he hadn't. He'd wanted *her* to come to *him*. Instead, he'd gotten a slap in the face with that suggestive dance she'd been doing, practically begging to be part of their ménage. Had she realized it? Or was she innocent?

Regardless, the ball was in her court once more. If she didn't call this time, he'd seek her out. Since he knew where she lived, it wasn't like she could hide from him. He'd give her two weeks tops, and then he'd go after her. With roses in hand if necessary. Anything to convince her to give him another chance.

Chapter Three

Every day for the next two weeks, she stared at the card sitting on her coffee table. It seemed that Alex was a motorcycle mechanic at a local shop, one that wasn't too far from her apartment. She'd handled the card so much the edges were starting to wear down. She'd picked up the phone several times, ready to call him, but for some reason had always chickened out. What if he didn't really want to see her again? What if he'd only been nice or had changed his mind? Just because they'd had two nights together hadn't meant anything.

But as she stared at the phone for the hundredth time, she realized she was either going to have to call or go visit. It couldn't be put off. She should have started her period and it hadn't come. So she'd bought a home pregnancy test. Four of them. And all four said the same thing -- she was pregnant. Since she hadn't been careless with anyone else, it had to be Alex's baby. But how was she going to convince him of that? For that matter, did she really need to? Women raised babies on their own all the time.

She paced in her living room and glanced at the phone again. There really wasn't any reason to tell him. He didn't seem like the kind of guy to be tied down by a woman and a kid, so why would he want to know she was pregnant?

On the other hand, he should be given the opportunity to be a part of his son's, or daughter's life. She was damned if she did and damned if she didn't. Making up her mind to do it, to just go ahead and confront him, in person, and just get it over with, she rushed to the bedroom and threw on a pair of cutoff shorts and a tank top before brushing out her long purple streaked hair. She slipped on a pair of flip-flops and hurried out the door before she could change her mind.

She got in her VW Bug and drove to the shop. When she pulled in and got out, she received more than one wolf whistle, but there was only one guy she wanted to see. She spotted him almost immediately and when he saw her, he gave her that slow sexy smile that had turned her knees to Jell-O the first moment she'd met him.

"Bailey, what a pleasant surprise. I was starting to think you'd never call me."

"Yeah, well... I've thought about it a few times, but I wasn't sure what to say."

He quirked an eyebrow. "And you figured it out today?"

"Not exactly. Today I'm here more out of... well, not necessity, but duty. Can we talk for a minute?"

"Sure." He motioned for her to follow him around the side of the building where there was a table with a few chairs.

After they sat, Bailey began to fidget. Now that she was here, she didn't know how to tell him. How did you tell a guy you barely knew that he was going to be a father? Blurting it out didn't seem the right way to go about it. The easiest perhaps, but she didn't want to send him into shock. Well, no more than was necessary.

"So to what do I owe the pleasure of this visit?" he asked.

"You aren't going to find it so pleasant."

He frowned. "Why not?"

"Do you remember our two nights together?"

"Of course. How could I forget?"

"Um... do you remember that we forgot something rather important both times?" she asked.

"I'm not following."

"A condom, Alex. We forgot to use a condom."

His face blanked and he stared at her for a long moment. "Are you trying to tell me you're pregnant?"

"Yeah, I am. I don't expect anything from you," she said in a rush, "I just thought you might want to know. Telling you seemed like the right thing to do. I've struggled with it though. I started to just leave it alone, but then I thought... What if he's one of those guys who would actually want to be part of his child's life? So, here I am."

"My parents were such screw-ups that I never wanted kids."

"Then you won't hear from me again." She started to stand, but he quickly restrained her.

"I didn't say I didn't want to see you again. I just said I hadn't ever wanted kids. Obviously you being pregnant changes things. Whether I want them or not, I'm going to have one."

She shook her head. "You don't have to be part of our lives. I can take care of the baby on my own. I've already started researching doctors and I'm going to find a small house so I'll have plenty of room."

"You're going to move in with me."

Both of her eyebrows winged up. "Excuse me?"

"I have a house not too far from here. You'll move in with me. I don't just want to see the kid every other weekend and on rotating holidays. I want to do this right."

"Meaning what?"

"Meaning we'll live together."

Obviously marriage wasn't in the cards, which was fine with her. Marriage could complicate things even more than they already were. Living together would be a trial enough since they hardly knew one another. Not that she'd agreed to his outlandish idea.

Granted, it had its merits, but she didn't want to live with a complete stranger. Okay, so she knew how he liked to have his cock sucked, that he could get a little rough when he fucked, but that wasn't a good basis for a real relationship. They barely knew one another! Other than his name, and the fact that he worked as a motorcycle mechanic, what did she really know about him?

"I think we need to slow things down a bit," she said.

"I think we passed that point already."

"No, there's plenty of time. We need to get to know one another before we take that kind of step."

Alex shook his head. "I don't think you understand, Bailey. When I say I want to be there for my child's life, I mean from the beginning. As in now. I want to go with you to doctor's appointments, make late night ice cream runs, help you up off the sofa when you get too big to do it by yourself. By taking care of you, I'm taking care of the baby."

What he said made sense, but it didn't mean she had to like it. She didn't want to let someone in that much, not someone she didn't know. Casual sex was one thing, living with someone was something else. She wanted that level of commitment, but she knew that Alex wasn't the one to give it to her. She didn't want him doing this out of some misplaced sense of duty. She wanted a commitment from someone because they cared about her and wanted to be with her. Was that so wrong?

"When do you expect me to move in?"

"When is your lease up?"

"Not for another three months."

He shook his head. "If we're going to make this work, we need all the time together we can get before the baby gets here. Three months is too long. You'll have to break it. I'll come help you pack this weekend."

"This weekend? But that's only three days away!"

Alex stood. "Then you have plenty of time to contact your leasing office and let them know about your change in plans. Find out what you need to do to cancel your lease. If you have to pay anything, I'll help you with it."

She narrowed her eyes at him. "I'm more than capable of paying my own bills thank you very much."

"We'll discuss bills later. Right now I have to get back to work."

She stood. "Fine. But I'm paying my way."

Bailey followed him around to the front of the building where the other mechanics were eyeing them in curiosity. She could only imagine what he was going to tell them. If he told them the truth, he was bound to get grief over it. She had a feeling he was one of those super careful guys who always used protection so he wouldn't get trapped, and look what happened. Not that she was trapping him. Nope, he was doing that all by himself.

* * *

Alex's mind was blown. A baby. Never in a million years did he think he'd be a father. He wasn't quite sure what to make of it, but he knew he'd made the right decision. If their child was going to have a normal life, with two loving, devoted parents, they needed to move in together. It was the only thing that made sense. Bouncing a child between two households wouldn't be easy and would only be confusing for the child later. He knew there were plenty of kids that came from broken homes, but he refused to let his be one of them.

Oddly, knowing his days of hitting the clubs and working his way through the eligible women in town was at an end didn't really bother him. Maybe because he hadn't been with anyone but Bailey since the night they met. He wasn't sure if he should tell her that or not. Would it make a difference?

When he returned to the motorcycle he was working on, the guys all gave him knowing smiles. Bailey was the first and only woman to show up at his work place. Hell, she was the only one who knew where he worked. Even from the start she'd been different. He'd never given his business card to a quick lay before, and maybe he'd given it to her because he'd known she was going to be more than that.

A baby. By all rights, he should feel terrified right now, but the thought of Bailey swollen with his child made him smile. For someone who'd forsworn marriage and all the trappings that went with it, he was handling the news very well. If it had been anyone else, any woman other than Bailey, he couldn't say for sure that he would've reacted as well. No, if it had been any woman other than Bailey, he would have sent her on her way, as horrible as that might sound.

No, he was with Bailey because that's where he was supposed to be. The only woman who'd made him want more than just one night. Maybe things were going to be okay after all.

Chapter Four

After her visit with Alex, Bailey went home and paced in her small apartment. Had she done the right thing? Just because he was offering to help didn't mean it was the right thing to do. Now she had to face him day in and day out, a near stranger. Living with him would be difficult.

She looked around the place she'd called home for the past few years and sighed. She didn't want to pack and move, but it seemed Alex wasn't giving her much of a choice. What was she going to do with him? She'd tried to refuse, but he'd just plowed right over her. He was definitely a domineering man. But then, she should've expected that. She'd always been attracted to alpha males.

Her attraction to him was going to be the only plus of moving in with him. Assuming he still wanted to have anything to do with her after today.

How did she feel about it? She bit her lip. As crazy as it sounded, the idea of sleeping in his arms every night held great appeal. And if she was warming his bed, she knew he wouldn't stray to someone else's. She realized that was going to be important to her. They needed to set some ground rules. If they were going to live together, they weren't going to date other people. She'd have to make that clear to him, just in case it wasn't understood already.

She went to her office and emailed her work contacts, letting them know she would have a change of address for them by Monday. Bailey knew she needed to call her mother, but she just couldn't bring herself to do so yet. Not only did she not want to explain to her very conservative mother that she was moving in with a man, but that she was going to have his child without the benefit of marriage. It just wasn't something she was ready to tackle yet. She had plenty of time before she had to make that call.

Picking up the phone, she called her friend Mia to tell her the latest turn her life had taken. She knew her friend would have good advice for her. Honestly, she should have talked to her before going to see Alex, but hadn't really thought about it. She'd wanted to make the decision on her own.

When Mia didn't answer, Bailey left her a message to call her as soon as she could, no matter what time it was. She knew her friend would worry after receiving such a cryptic message, but she hadn't wanted to leave the details over voicemail. Mia had been there for her when she'd lost her father eight years ago, when she'd lost her fiancé two years after that, and when she'd gone into a downward spiral of alcohol and drugs shortly thereafter. It was Mia who had pulled her back up and gotten her back on the right path. If it weren't for her friend, there was no telling what might have happened to her.

At twenty-seven, she should be ready for a home, husband, and children. But instead, she'd just been looking for a stable relationship. It had taken her a while to grow up after the tragic events in her life and for the longest time she'd just wanted to have fun and experience all that life had to offer. But now it was time to grow up. Whether she was ready or not, she was going to be a mom. The thought terrified her. What if she screwed up? What if she was a horrible parent? Her own mother wasn't exactly a stellar example to go by.

Picking up the card on the table, she fiddled with it a moment. Chewing on a corner of her nail, she dialed the number and asked to speak with Alex. She knew she should give him more time to wrap his head around everything, but she was a planner, and until things were more settled between them she wouldn't be able to rest easy.

"Bailey? Is something wrong?" he asked when came on the line.

"I'm okay. I just… Can we talk? When you get off work?"

He was silent a moment. "After I run home and shower, I'll pick you up for dinner. How does that sound?"

"As long as we can talk, that will be fine."

"I'll see you in a few hours."

She disconnected the call and set the phone down on the table beside the business card. She felt a little better knowing that some of her questions would be answered, her concerns laid to rest. Unless his answers just caused her to have even more cause for concern. No, she would think positive. And in the meantime, she would take a relaxing bath and try to clear her mind.

*　*　*

Bailey was dressed in one of her more conservative outfits. She'd put on her black Capri pants and teal blouse with a pair of black ballet flats. With her hair pulled back in a pretty clip, and a light layer of make-up on, she was ready to tackle the world -- or at least Alex. She hoped.

When a knock sounded at her door, butterflies erupted in her stomach. He was here. With a shaky hand, she opened the door. He'd put on a pair of dark wash jeans and a navy button down shirt. With his hair still slightly damp from his shower, he was mouthwatering. He was clean shaven and the hint of his aftershave hung in the air, teasing her.

His gaze skimmed her from head to toe and his lips tipped up in a grin.

"You look nice," he said.

"Thanks. You do, too."

His grin broadened. Holding out his hand, he asked, "Shall we?"

She snagged her purse and accepted his hand. Pulling the door shut behind her, she locked up and let him escort her down to his car. She was thankful he'd brought the Mustang and not his motorcycle.

The ride to the restaurant was a quiet one, and Bailey fretted over what she would say to Alex once they reached their destination. She knew *what* she wanted to say. She just wasn't sure *how* to say it. What if she was worrying for nothing? What if he had the same ideas she did, and she was just going to sound paranoid?

She tried to calm her mind and enjoy the ride. When they pulled up in front of The Roadhouse, she was pleasantly surprised. A steak and potato would hit the spot. And the casual atmosphere would set her at ease. She shouldn't feel so nervous around him. They'd had sex twice! But then, she didn't really know him, did she? Just because they'd been intimate didn't mean she knew anything about Alex.

He parked the car and they headed inside. It wasn't a busy night so they were seated right away. After they'd perused their menus and given their orders to the waitress, Bailey fidgeted.

"You sounded upset on the phone earlier," Alex said, studying her intently.

"I just… what are we doing, Alex? We're strangers. How on earth could we possibly think of living together?"

"So you want to get to know me before you move in? Is that it?"

"Yes. Well, partly."

He drummed his fingers on the table. "What else?"

"I'm assuming when you said we would live together, you meant long-term."

"Of course I meant long-term. We're going to raise a child together, Bailey. Did you think I only meant while the child was an infant?"

"It's just…" She bit her lip, not sure how to proceed.

"What is it that has you so rattled?"

"Do you plan to see other women while we're living together?" There. She'd said it.

He looked surprised by her question. "Bailey, what did you think I meant when I said you would be moving in with me?"

"I wasn't really sure. Honestly, it's had me rather agitated all afternoon."

His gaze softened. "I didn't mean to upset you when I brought it up. After our two rather incredible nights together, I had thought that answer would be rather obvious. You'll share my bed as well as my home, and you'll be the only woman in my life."

"But you haven't made a commitment before, nor wanted a relationship, that I know of. Can you just flip a switch and suddenly change? How do I know you won't…"

"Stray?"

She nodded.

"Because I give you my word. Not only will I be faithful to you, but I'll expect the same in return."

"I was actually looking for a relationship when I met you."

His eyebrow lifted.

"What?" she demanded.

"Dressed as you were?"

"What was wrong with the way I was dressed?"

"Honey, you were dressed like you were looking for a good time, not a steady relationship."

Her shoulders tensed. "I happen to think I looked nice that night."

"Oh, you looked nice all right. You looked even better once I had you out of that scrap of fabric you called a dress. Speaking of, plan on burning all of those dresses."

Her mouth dropped open. "I beg your pardon?"

"I'm not going to have my woman walking around with her body on display advertising it's for sale."

She narrowed her eyes. Just because she'd thought of buying new clothes didn't mean he got to dictate to her what she could and couldn't wear. "I happen to like my clothes. If you have a problem with my wardrobe, it's *your* problem. Not mine. I'll dress however I damn well please."

"You're going to be a mother. Why can't you dress more like are you are now? You look nice tonight."

"You wouldn't have looked twice at me if I'd dressed this way."

"That's the point, Bailey. I'm the only one who should be looking at you. Besides, you'll be buying maternity clothes before long. I doubt those come in micro-mini skirts."

"Then there's no reason I can't enjoy my clothes until then. Besides, I doubt I'll be going to the club much. It isn't like I can go drinking, now can I? Who's going to see me lying around the house in cut-off shorts and tank tops?"

"No, I guess you can't. You can still dance though."

She sighed. "We're off topic."

"I don't think so."

"Basically, you're expecting all of the benefits of marriage, including bossing me around, without an actual marriage. Am I getting this right?"

He looked slightly uncomfortable at the mention of the word marriage. "Yeah. I don't see the need for us to get married."

"I didn't say I wanted to get married. I'm just making sure I have all of my facts straight."

Their food arrived, interrupting their conversation. Bailey decided to let the matter rest while they ate. Instead, she asked questions about Alex so she could get to know him a little better. In return, she told him about her work. Then the conversation got a little uncomfortable again.

"So let me ask you something," he said. "If you were looking for a stable relationship, why were you such a party girl?"

"I like to have a good time. Is that a crime?"

"No, it just doesn't seem to fit. You're what, twenty-five?"

"Twenty-seven."

He looked surprised. "And you haven't been in a stable relationship before?"

"I was once. It...things...something happened, something bad."

"What happened?"

"I'd rather not talk about it," she said.

"If this is going to work between us, we have to be open and honest with each other, Bailey."

"He died, okay?" She turned to stare out the window as painful memories swamped her.

"I'm sorry," Alex said quietly. "If I had known, I wouldn't have pushed you."

"We were engaged to be married. It was just three weeks before our wedding. He'd called to tell me he had a surprise for me and would be late getting home. But several hours later, it wasn't Josh at the front door, it was the police. A drunk driver had plowed into my fiancé on his way home, killing him instantly. They also found the remains of a puppy in the car, my surprise."

She looked at him with tears swimming in her eyes. "You might as well know, I hit a downward spiral after that. I started drinking heavily, and when that couldn't dull the pain anymore, I turned to drugs. My friend Mia was finally able to pull me back out, dragging me kicking and screaming into the land of the living. If it weren't for her, I'd probably be dead by now. When Josh died, all I wanted to do was join him. My whole world was ripped apart and nothing could put it back together again. When I drank, at least I was able to forget for a little while."

"I can't tell you how sorry I am, Bailey. No one should have to go through that."

"The funny thing is that if Josh had lived, I probably would have been a mother twice over by now. And yet, here I am, pregnant and terrified that I'm going to screw it up somehow."

"You won't screw it up, honey. You're going to do just fine."

She blinked back tears as his hand reached for hers. His thumb gently caressed her hand as he gazed at her tenderly.

"I'd already guessed you were a strong woman, but now, knowing what you've been through, I have to say that you absolutely amaze me. Sitting here with you tonight, I have to wonder how I got so lucky to have a woman like you in my life. We might not have chosen our path, but I can't think of anyone I'd rather have by my side. You're really something.

"I'm not saying that things are going to be easy. I've never lived with anyone before, and it's been a really long time for you. It's going to be a lot of give and take, and I imagine we'll flounder from time to time. But if we work together, I think we're going to do well.

"You haven't asked a lot about me, and I haven't volunteered much. I don't have any tragic stories, a reason for why I am the way I am. Well, that's not entirely true. I guess you can blame my series of one night stands on my last serious girlfriend, Monica Ersald. We dated junior and senior year of high school, until I found out she'd been cheating on me with my best friend. That was the last serious relationship I had, the last time I let a woman in past one night."

He squeezed her hand. "So, me asking you... all right, me *telling* you to move in, isn't something I would normally do. And I didn't do it strictly because of the baby. After being with you, I know that I could wake up next to you every morning and not want to stray. I know that you'll be enough, you and the baby. So while things may be rough from time to time, always remember that I'm choosing you and our child."

Tears clogged her throat. No one had ever said anything so wonderful to her before. It made her think that just maybe they had a chance to make this work.

Alex paid the check and took Bailey home.

***

At her apartment, he drew her into his arms and held her close. Part of her wanted to pull away, but instead she found herself burrowing into him. Having his arms around her felt nice, secure. After dredging up all of those old memories of Josh, she felt raw and emotionally drained.

She looked at him and the tenderness in his eyes was nearly her undoing. Something had happened between them at dinner, something had changed. They still didn't know one another very well, yet somehow they were closer. She no longer felt apprehensive about moving in with him. If anything, she found herself looking forward to it. The thought of lying in his arms night after night sounded heavenly.

Alex lowered his head and kissed her gently. His lips caressed hers in the softest of kisses, different from anything they'd shared before. As his tongue entered her mouth to taste her, she clung to him, not trusting her legs to hold her up. He kissed her slowly, as if savoring the moment. Everything up to this point had been wild and reckless with them. Now it seemed he wanted to take his time.

He trailed kisses along her jaw and nipped her ear. "Let me love you tonight," he whispered.

Her heart stuttered in her chest at his word choice. She knew he couldn't possibly mean that he loved her, it would be too good to be true, but oh how she wished that he did, that he could. She had no doubt that love was not going to be part of their arrangement, and it broke her heart.

The desire in his eyes had her reaching up to slowly unbutton his shirt. Tugging it free from his jeans, she slid it down his arms to puddle on the floor at their feet. Alex lifted her into his arms and carried her down the hall.

"We're doing this the right way this time. Which room is yours?"

"Straight ahead."

He pushed the bedroom door open and gently laid her down on the unmade bed. With infinite care, he undressed her, taking his time, drawing out the process. When he unbuttoned the last button on her blouse, he pushed it open, caressing her skin along the way. Unfastening her pants, he slid them down her legs and tossed them onto the chair that sat in the corner of the small room. Sitting before him in nothing but her bra and panties, she shivered.

"Cold?" he asked.

She shook her head. No, she was hot. So very hot. Her skin felt like it was on fire, burning for his touch. She wanted him so much she ached for his touch, his kiss. Biting her tongue, she barely refrained from begging him to take her.

He unfastened her bra and slid the straps down her shoulders. Her nipples pebbled under his gaze, asking to be touched. Alex leaned forward and gently captured one in his mouth, sucking the sensitive tip. She buried her hands in his hair, urging him on, never wanting him to stop. His tongue swirled over the pointed nub and she grew even wetter. When he pulled away, she cried out at the loss.

He kissed her neck and eased her back down onto the bed. His hands caressed her sides as his fingers trailed down to her hips. Grasping her panties, he gently tugged them down her legs, dropping them on the floor.

Lying before him naked, she felt even more ready than before. As his heated gaze devoured her, she reached for him, needing to feel him against her. Alex stood and divested himself of the remainder of his clothes before lying down beside her. He cupped one of her breasts and stroked his thumb over her nipple.

"Have I ever told you how beautiful you are?" he asked, his voice husky with desire.

"No, I don't think you have."

"You are. You're one of the most beautiful women I've ever seen." He stroked one of her purple streaks. "Even with these."

"And you are, without a doubt, the most handsome man I've ever seen. Even though I didn't call after our first time together, I thought about you every day."

"So why didn't you call?"

"I didn't want to seem needy."

He grinned and leaned down to kiss her. "I never would have thought you were needy. I thought about you, too."

Her heart thrilled at his words.

Alex kissed her neck, softly sucking the tender skin, leaving his mark on her before moving on. He trailed kisses across her breasts before latching onto a nipple. He sucked and licked the hardened nub until her pussy was aching to be filled. Then he moved over to the other one and gave it the same treatment, teasing and tormenting her some more. He kissed his way down her stomach, settling between her thighs. She gripped the sheets as he licked her slit, fighting the urge to wrap her legs around him.

Alex dipped his tongue inside of her before circling her clit. The bundle of nerves was begging to be touched, but his tongue skirted around it, driving her mad. She lifted her hips, a silent plea. His tongue delved inside of her again making her squirm. Heat suffused her body from head to toe, the flames of desire licking her skin. Her nipples throbbed as his tongue plunged into her again and again. Just when she thought she couldn't take any more, his tongue circled her clit before swiping over it. She gasped at the contact, then he sucked the sensitive nub into his mouth and she came, crying out as wave after wave of pleasure rolled over her.

His mouth was relentless, taking her to new heights as another orgasm took her to the next level. He grabbed the cheeks of her ass and pulled her tight against him, his mouth sucking and licking until she came down from her high.

When she lay replete, he kissed her inner thigh before licking and kissing his way back up her body. He claimed her mouth in a searing kiss, and she tasted her essence on his tongue. His lips were demanding and she gave him everything she had, turning her control over to him completely, letting him be her master in every way.

She felt his cock against her wet folds and she wrapped her legs around his waist, begging for him to take her. She felt empty and needed to be filled with him, needed him more than she'd ever needed anyone before. The head of his cock teased her and she whimpered, lifting her hips, trying to take him inside of her. He rubbed the head of his cock over her clit before sliding into her wet heat, burying himself to the hilt. She practically purred in satisfaction. The delicious friction of his cock moving in and out of her made her skin hum. She lifted her hips, taking him in deeper and he moaned before claiming her lips with his. With him filling her senses, she let go, coming in a mind-blowing orgasm that left her shaking. Alex thrust into her deeply one last time, coming inside of her.

He kissed her softly, tenderly, his lips a gentle caress against hers. "Are you all right?" he asked.

"I'm wonderful." She smiled and caressed his cheek.

He rolled to his side and pulled her into his arms, kissing the top of her head. She could hear his heart thundering in his chest and she snuggled into him. Their bodies were slick with sweat, but she didn't care. Being in Alex's arms was all that mattered because she realized that she had done the impossible, the unthinkable, the worst thing ever... she had fallen in love with him. She knew he would break her heart, but that didn't matter. It seemed that not only her body wanted him, her heart did too.

They lay entwined in one another's arms for a while, but eventually Alex pulled away. "I have to be at work early tomorrow."

"So you're leaving?"

He kissed her. "It won't be long before I'll be staying with you all night. If I had realized we would end up sleeping together tonight, I would have brought a change of clothes."

She stood and walked to the closet, grabbing her robe from inside. Slipping the silky garment on, she belted it and faced him. "I understand."

He rose and pulled her into his arms. "I'll be here bright and early Saturday to help you pack, all right?"

She nodded.

Alex dressed quickly and she followed him to the front door. After another sweet kiss, she let him out and locked up behind him.

She didn't know what had changed between them tonight, but something had. Whatever it was, she was thankful for it. She was getting to see a softer, gentler side to the man she was about to spend her life with. It set her at ease about moving in with him, made her look forward to it even.

Moving down the hall, she entered the bathroom and started the shower. She felt sticky, but in a good way. Stepping under the warm water, she washed quickly. Alex might not be coming until Saturday to help her pack, but she still had plans to make before then, and the sooner she got started the better off she'd be.

Bailey got out of the shower and dried off. She went into the bedroom and put on a clean pair of panties and her favorite pair of pajamas. The first thing she needed to do was start a list of things she would need that Alex may or may not have, like wireless internet for her work and a space for her home office. It was important to her to have a quiet space to work. Well, quiet might not be an accurate term to use. She had a tendency to blast rock music when she worked, but it helped her focus.

She also needed to figure out what to do with her furniture. She assumed that Alex already had furniture at his place so he wouldn't need hers. She wouldn't part with her desk and chair in her office, but she had no clue what to do with the rest of it. Donate it maybe? It was another thing to add to the list of questions to ask Alex.

Whether he had room in his kitchen or not, she was taking her pots and pans with her. She'd bought an expensive set when she'd moved several years ago, and she refused to part with it. Her plates and glasses she didn't care about, but it was yet another item to discuss with him. She had known that moving in with him would be a big deal, but she hadn't thought about all of the extra things, like furniture, that went along with it.

Picking up her Nook, she settled in bed to read for the night. She'd just downloaded a copy of *Anna Doubles Down* that morning and she couldn't wait to read it. A western ménage was just what she needed to finish off her night.

* * *

All of Alex's senses were alive, and they were all still trained on Bailey. He knew he needed to go home and shower before bed, but he wasn't ready to wash away her scent. He couldn't wait to lie down at night and have her by his side.

He'd learned so much about her tonight. When he'd seen the tears gathered in her eyes at the restaurant, he'd wanted to take her in his arms and kiss away her sorrow. He'd never wanted to comfort a woman on that level before.

When she'd talked about a fiancé, his heart had ached. Not so much for her loss, but the thought that they might've never met. They may not have known one another for very long, but already she was important to him.

And then later, the way she'd come apart in his arms... he'd never experienced anything like it before. He'd pleased countless women over the years, but none of them mattered. Only Bailey, with her flashing eyes and sparkling smile, had ever managed to matter to him. He hadn't had a serious girlfriend since high school. It seemed right that Bailey should have the honor of being his first, and only, serious adult relationship. Knowing that they would be raising a child together, he felt it was safe to say that he'd live out the rest of his days with Bailey by his side. At least, he was starting to hope that's what would happen.

Chapter Five

By the time Saturday rolled around, Bailey had managed to pack most of her clothes and shoes, her pots and pans, and all of her pictures and books -- which was saying a lot because she had a *ton* of books. With a few changes of clothes, her Nook, and her make-up stashed in an overnight bag, she was ready to pack everything else.

Alex knocked on the door at eight in the morning, startling Bailey. He'd said he was coming early, but she hadn't expected him quite that early. She was still in her pajamas and hadn't finished her coffee yet. Opening the door, she peeked around the edge at him.

"Ready to pack?" he asked with a smile.

"Um. Sort of."

She opened the door wider so he could come in. When he saw what she was wearing, his eyebrows lifted.

"Not a morning person?" he asked.

She shook her head. "Not really. I just got up a few minutes ago. Let me finish my coffee and I'll get dressed. I'm afraid I'm used to sleeping until nine or so. I'm more of a night owl."

He noticed the boxes stacked along the hall and frowned. "I thought we were packing you up this weekend."

"We are. I just decided to get a head start on some things. And I made a list of things I wasn't sure about." She picked up a piece of paper from the coffee table and handed it to him.

He skimmed over it quickly and set it aside.

"I have four bedrooms. One for us, one for the baby, one is set up as a guest room and another as an office. The office is rather large so if you want to put your desk in there, there's plenty of room for it. I cleared out the baby's room over the past few days. I thought you might want to shop for baby furniture one day soon."

"Well... you've just thought of everything, haven't you?"

"Not quite. As to your furniture... we don't really need it. My bed is bigger than yours and so is my sofa. If you want to keep your living room TV, we can mount it on the wall in the bedroom."

"I guess I'll have to rent a truck to take the furniture somewhere and donate it."

"Call Goodwill. They'll come pick it up. Tell them if they want it, they need to come today or tomorrow. We can bag up your bedding and anything you aren't taking and have everything ready."

"What about my dishes?"

"You can bring them if you want. There's space for them. Just pack up the whole kitchen. Same with your bathroom. You'll only need to donate the furniture and bedding. Everything else can go."

"How are we getting all of this to your house?"

"I'm renting a truck tomorrow and the guys from the shop are going to help me move everything."

She bit her lip. "What did you tell them?"

"That my girlfriend was moving in."

"And they didn't think you were crazy? As far as they're concerned, I didn't even exist in your world until I told you about the baby a few days ago."

He grinned. "There might have been a few comments, but nothing I couldn't handle. Besides, I told them you were pregnant and that shut them up. I don't think any of them knew what to think of me being a dad."

"I've only told my friend Mia that I'm pregnant. I have no idea what to say to my mother. I haven't even told her that I'm moving. For that matter, I don't know that I *will* tell her that I'm moving."

He gave her a funny look. "You don't think she'll notice?"

"Thankfully she doesn't live here. I guess she'll wonder why my phone doesn't work anymore after this weekend." She sighed.

"So why don't you want to tell your mother?"

"She's very conservative and overly religious. I'd have to hear a lecture about going to hell if she heard I was moving in with you, much less that we're having a baby together. Trust me, it isn't something she's going to be happy about. It's best if she doesn't know she's going to be a grandmother."

Alex frowned. "You have to tell her sometime."

"You didn't hear all of the hateful things she said when Josh and I moved in together. And we were engaged! No, just no. I'm not telling her. Not now anyway."

"All right. But just for the record, I don't agree with your decision."

She nodded. Having finished her coffee, she got up and walked down the hall toward the bedroom. "I'm just going to change and then I can get started on sorting and packing."

"Take your time. I'm going to bring up the boxes I picked up yesterday."

Bailey changed quickly, stuffing her pajamas in her overnight bag. Before Alex was back with his armful of boxes, she had started digging out her bedding and stuffing it into garbage bags to be donated. Next, she stripped the bed and threw everything in the washer. If she was going to donate it, the least she could do was make sure it was clean.

She called Goodwill and set up a time for them to pick up her donations. That would give her plenty of time to get things together.

Alex came back and dropped an armload of boxes in the living room. He locked up and turned to face her. "What did you want to tackle first?"

"Would you mind packing the kitchen? I can work on the bathroom while you do that."

He nodded. "You know, you never told me what the leasing office said."

"I forfeit my deposit and have to pay next month's rent in order to break my contract."

"I'll take care of the rent. It's the least I can do since I insisted you move in immediately."

"You know, I can afford to pay my own bills."

He grinned and pulled her close. Bending his head, he kissed her. "I know you can, but we're in this together from this point forward. I'm the reason you're breaking your lease so it only makes sense that I pay the penalty for it. We can discuss bills later."

"I'm helping you make the house payments, and I won't argue about it."

He just shook his head. "I hate to be the one to break it to you, but there are no monthly payments on the house. I bought it at auction and fixed it up. I own it free and clear."

Her mouth dropped open. How on earth did a motorcycle mechanic afford to do something like that? For that matter, how did he afford that expensive Harley and car that he seemed to pamper? There was a lot about Alex that she didn't know.

Bailey wasn't broke by any means, but there was no way she could pay cash for a house. She had enough in savings that she could have put a down payment on one, but that's about it. Most of her money had gone into her home office. She had a state of the art laptop loaded with expensive software, a rather pricey desk and chair, and a top of the line all-in-one printer. She hadn't spared any expense when it came to her work.

While Alex banged around in the kitchen, she started on the bathroom. She only owned a handful of towels so they were quick and easy to pack. It was all of her bath products that took forever. It was amazing how much you accumulated in a few years time. She had more shower gel, bubble bath and bath salts than she would ever know what to do with, and yet she couldn't make herself part with any of it. She only hoped Alex had a large bathroom with lots of cabinet space. When she was finished with the bathroom, she stretched her back and went to the kitchen for a soda.

"What are you doing?" Alex asked as she pulled a can out of the refrigerator.

"Getting something to drink. Want one?"

"You can't have that."

She frowned. "Why not?"

"You already had coffee today. Too much caffeine isn't good for the baby."

"And how would you know?"

"Because I did some reading the last couple of days. You should drink more water, juice and milk."

She gripped the can tighter. "I'm having a soda and there's nothing you can do about it. I doubt that one little soda is going to harm the baby."

"Fine. But the next thing you drink should be healthy for you."

Bailey popped the top on the can and guzzled half of it down. She sat it on the kitchen counter and motioned toward the plates in the open cabinet.

"You don't have to pack those. I'm not attached to them."

"You want to donate them?" he asked.

"Sure. I'll just stick them on the bed with the rest of the stuff that's going away. I'm sure you have more than enough plates and glasses. Flatware, too. I won't need any of that stuff."

"You're out of luck on the glasses. I already packed them."

She nodded. "That's fine. I'll just donate the other things then. I'd like to take my cooking utensils though."

"I'll get that packed next, and then we can start on your bedroom."

"I'm actually heading that way now. I've already finished with the bathroom."

"We'll pack your bedroom and office and then do another sweep through the apartment to make sure we didn't miss anything. After that, we'll empty your refrigerator and take the trash out. Then we'll just have to meet Goodwill this afternoon and move everything tomorrow and we'll be finished."

"Except for unpacking."

"Yes, but you can take your time doing that. There's no rush."

"Then let's get to it."

* * *

Later that afternoon, Bailey watched as the last of her donated items were carried out of her apartment. She'd thought she would feel something, watching her possessions walk away like that, but she didn't. All she felt was tired. But then she'd noticed that she tired easily these days. She had a doctor's appointment set for early in the week and hoped the doctor would be able to help her out. She prayed she wasn't coming down with a bug in addition to being pregnant. She'd started feeling queasy and had even thrown up a few times, not that she'd told Alex that. The last thing she needed was for him to start worrying. Maybe she should purchase one of those pregnancy books next time she was in the store. Not having been around any pregnant women before, she really was clueless as to what to expect.

With nowhere to sit, she leaned against the wall and closed her eyes.

"Tired?" Alex asked softly.

"A little."

He brushed her hair back from her face. "Let's go home so you can get some rest. I'll fill the tub with some warm water and you can soak for a while if you'd like."

"That sounds heavenly. Steaming water would be divine."

"You can't have steaming water, it wouldn't be good for the baby."

She groaned. "I'm starting to wonder why women get pregnant. It sounds like a very miserable time to me. No steaming hot baths, no caffeine… anything else I should know about?"

"Well, you can feel more tired than usual."

She sighed.

"Come on. Let's get you home."

She leaned down to pick up her bag, but Alex beat her to it. As tired as she was, she didn't argue and let him carry it. Locking up the apartment, she followed him down to his car. It was a fairly short drive to his house. To say she was surprised by the structure was an understatement. The two story white brick home was beautiful. The front yard was landscaped with azaleas and an assortment of colorful flowers, the grass a vibrant green and completely weed free. It was obvious that he took care of his home.

They pulled into the double garage, and the first thing Bailey noticed was the missing motorcycle. She wondered where he kept it if not at his home. Surely he didn't keep it at work.

"We'll bring your car home tomorrow," he told her. "I'll get the second garage door opener for you."

"But... isn't that where you keep your bike?"

He gave her a sad smile. "Not anymore."

"What do you mean?" she asked with a frown.

"I'm selling it."

"But, why? Why would you do that?"

He shrugged. "With a baby on the way it just didn't seem like something practical to own. I can put a car seat in the Mustang if I need to, and we'll have your car..."

"I sense a but in there."

"How attached are you to your Bug?"

She narrowed her eyes. "Why?"

"It doesn't have a lot of room in the backseat, and neither does the Mustang. I just thought it might make sense for one of us to have a car with a little more room. How do you feel about SUVs?"

Without answering, she got out of the car and slammed the door. Not even in his house yet and he was already dictating another aspect of her life. All right, so he had a good point, and he was making sacrifices by sharing his home with her and selling his motorcycle. If she were honest with herself, she'd admit that it *would* make more sense for her to have a vehicle with more room. But that didn't mean she had to agree with him right now. Besides, she'd rather keep her savings to use for the baby than as a down payment on another vehicle.

She stepped through the door into a laundry room. Moving through the door to the left, she entered the kitchen. A large and airy room with lots of windows. The cabinets were a dark cherry and the floor was a dark natural stone. Granite counter tops gleamed. A cherry table that sat six dominated the breakfast nook, surrounded by windows overlooking what appeared to be the backyard.

Through an archway, she found herself in a formal dining room that opened to a living room. The furniture didn't look very well used so she had to assume it was a formal room used for special guests, or for looks only. So far, she was not only impressed with Alex's home, but very much surprised.

The living room opened to the front entry and a large staircase. On the other side of the stairs was another room, a family room that looked very much lived in. The leather furniture looked inviting, and she was certain that the large flat screen TV and wall of movies were used often.

She turned around and bumped into Alex. He reached out to steady her. "Are you ready to see the upstairs?"

She nodded.

He took her hand and led her up the staircase to the second floor. Stopping at the first room on the right, he pushed the door open and tugged her inside, setting her bag down on the floor.

"This is our room."

She looked around. The room was done in chocolate and beige, very tasteful, but nowhere near bright enough for her. Bailey wondered if he would have a problem with her redecorating a little. She glanced around again. The chocolate could stay, but maybe accent with aqua instead of beige. Something to add a little color to the otherwise drab room.

He pulled her back out of the room and opened the next door. The room was empty, the walls a plain eggshell color. Like the master bedroom, the floor was a dark wood that gleamed as if it had been freshly cleaned.

"I thought this could be the baby's room. We can either wait and paint it after you know if it's a boy or a girl, or we can paint it something neutral, like yellow," he said.

"I'm too overwhelmed to think about it today."

He led her down the hall to the next room. Pushing the door open, he showed her a third bedroom. There was a full size bed on one wall with a blue and white bedspread, along with a dresser and nightstand. Two windows looked out over the house next door. The walls were a tranquil blue.

"The guest room?" she guessed.

He nodded. "And last but not least," he said as he guided her to the final door on the hall, "the office."

Bailey stepped into the large room and looked around. He had been right. There was enough room for her desk along with his. She walked around the room, trying to envision where she would place her things. There was room along the wall by the windows. Her desk could easily fit there, and there would be just enough room on the side wall for her small credenza where she kept her files, iPod docking station and printer. All in all, the room would work nicely.

Alex pulled her back down the hall to the master bedroom.

"Why don't you soak in the tub and I'll figure out dinner? I know you're tired and I'm sure your muscles are sore."

"A soak in the tub sounds wonderful."

He ushered her into the bathroom where she was faced with the delightful sight of a large jetted tub big enough for two. She only wished she had her bubble bath or bath salts. But everything was packed in boxes back in her apartment. She would just have to make do with plain water.

Alex began filling the tub and pulled a large fluffy towel out of a built-in cabinet in the wall. After he made sure she had everything she needed, he leaned down to kiss her sweetly on the lips. Bailey wrapped her arms around his waist and leaned into him.

"Bailey, if you don't stop…"

"What?"

"There will be consequences."

She glanced at the tub. "There's room enough for two."

Slowly, he lifted her shirt over her head and dropped it on the floor. He cupped her lace covered breasts in his hands, stroking the nipples with his thumbs. Her nipples puckered, as if asking for more attention.

Bailey shimmied out of her shorts and panties. Reaching behind her back, she unfastened her bra. Alex slid the straps down her arms and let the garment fall to the floor. Standing before him completely bare, she ached for his touch.

Alex quickly stripped out of his clothes and pulled her into his arms. With their bodies pressed close together, she felt electrified, every nerve in her body completely aware of him. He lifted her into his arms and stepped into the tub. Sitting down with her in his lap, he turned off the water.

She turned to straddle him and he cupped her breasts, bringing them to his mouth. His lips closed over first one nipple and then the other, sucking and tugging on the peaks until she was moaning for more. She slid her fingers into his hair, holding him close. His cock bobbed in the water between them, and she reached down to stroke it.

He kissed her deeply, his tongue tangling with hers. With the heat of his lips on hers, she slowly sank onto his cock, taking him inside her pussy. When he filled her completely, she rocked her hips against him. Alex placed his hands on her hips, urging her on as she rode him, first slowly, then gradually moving faster and faster. The water in the tub sloshed around them as she fucked him. Just when she thought she couldn't take it another moment, they found their release together, clinging to one another.

"This wasn't quite what I had in mind when I told you to take a bath," he murmured against her hair.

She grinned and kissed him. "I think this was way better than a soak in the tub."

Alex cleaned her up and helped her out of the tub. Drying her off, he wrapped her in the fluffy towel and nudged her toward the bedroom. She got dressed while he was drying off, pulling on a tank and jean shorts. When Alex stepped into the bedroom, she watched as he pulled on a pair of boxers and jeans. As he headed toward the door, she realized he planned on leaving his shirt off, and she wondered if it was strictly to drive her crazy. The man was tempting enough with his clothes on.

Bailey followed him down the stairs to the kitchen. It was still early for dinner, but they hadn't eaten anything in hours and she was getting a little hungry. When she saw Alex pull some steaks out of the refrigerator, her mouth watered. He pulled out two potatoes from a bin in the pantry and wrapped them in foil. Next, she watched as he washed and seasoned the steaks.

"Is there anything I can do to help?" she asked.

He shook his head. "I'm just going to put the potatoes in the oven and cook the steaks out on the grill. I figure we'll eat in about an hour."

"Sounds good. I'm starving."

He frowned. "I can fix you a snack…"

"No, I'll be okay."

"You're eating for two now."

"I'm aware of that, but it won't kill me to wait an hour to eat."

He put the potatoes in the oven and put the steaks back in the refrigerator. After herding her into the family room, he turned on the TV and sat on the sofa, pulling her down beside him. He flipped through the channels until he found a comedy and then put the remote down.

Bailey curled into him and rested her head on his shoulder. If someone had told her a week ago that she would be cuddling with Alex Mendos on his living room sofa, she would have laughed. He just wasn't the type of guy Bailey had always pictured herself with. She'd seen him around, a different woman every time. But now… she had to admit that he had some good qualities. At first, he'd seemed stunned about the baby, not knowing quite what to say, other than to demand that she move in with him. She'd been skeptical, thinking it was a bad move for them to live together, virtual strangers. And yet, despite his overbearing ways, they got along fairly well. The sex was still beyond fabulous, but that wasn't enough of a basis for a relationship. She wasn't going to kid herself. She doubted that love would ever be part of their relationship, it was just too unconventional for that, but she had hopes that they could at least become great friends. Friends with benefits since she'd be sharing his bed.

Partway through the movie, Alex got up to finish making dinner. Bailey stayed on the sofa, watching the movie and thinking about her life.

Moving in with Alex was going to be a big change, but having a baby in her life was going to be an even bigger adjustment. She knew nothing about caring for an infant. What if she screwed up? She doubted Alex knew much more than she did, but maybe they could figure it out together.

Alex was a puzzle to her. He'd claimed to not want anything more than a one night stand, and yet, after their first time together, he'd offered her his number and said he wanted to see her again. And then, when he found out about the baby, he'd insisted she move in with him. Why was he acting so out of character? Had he just decided that he was ready to settle down and she was convenient, or was it something more than that? Could he possibly feel the same pull that she felt?

She had no idea why she felt so attracted to Alex. Sure, he was a divine kisser, an excellent dancer, beyond fantastic in bed, not to mention easy on the eyes... but it was something more than that. From the moment she'd laid eyes on him, something about him had called to her. She'd always been able to easily forget the men she'd slept with once she'd gotten them out of her system, but with Alex, she wasn't sure she would ever get tired of him. No matter how many times they were together, she always wanted him again. And every time they were together was even more incredible than the last.

Just thinking about his hard cock in her pussy made her wet. Remembering the feel of his mouth on her nipples made them pucker. She licked her lips at the thought of his cock sliding into her hot, wet mouth. She could practically taste him already.

A glance out the window showed that he was standing in the backyard at the grill, fixing their steaks. She eyed the yard thoughtfully. The fence was higher than your average privacy fence. It had to be at least seven feet tall, tall enough to hide them from prying eyes. A large pool dominated the middle of the yard, with a waterfall trickling into it from the middle of the left side. It was surrounded by natural stone and the left side was decorated with greenery and floral plants. It was a tropical paradise. And in much need of being christened to her way of thinking.

Bailey rose from the sofa and walked out to the backyard. Stepping off the deck onto the lower area where Alex stood, she began removing her clothes, slowly.

It took him a moment, but he finally noticed her and his eyebrows rose. "What are you doing?" he asked.

"Going for a swim."

He glanced at the pool and back at her. "You don't own a bathing suit?"

"Oh, I own one. But it's packed back at the apartment. Besides, it's just the two of us here. And it isn't like you haven't seen me naked before."

She dropped the last article of clothing in the grass and sashayed to the edge of the pool. Gracefully, she descended the stairs into the cool blue water. When she was waist deep, she turned to face him, beckoning him with the crook of her finger. "Why don't you come join me?"

He quickly moved the steaks to a plate on the side of the grill and began removing his clothes. In no time, he was naked and making his way toward her. She leaned back to wet her hair, and he reached out to cup her breasts, dragging his thumbs over her sensitive nipples. When she rose from the water, he claimed her mouth hungrily, his tongue diving between her lips for a taste. One hand cradled her head while the other splayed over her breast. He stroked her gently, making her nipples tighten even more.

She buried her hands in his hair, holding him to her as he ravaged her mouth. Arching against the hand on her breast, she begged him to touch her more. He plucked at her nipple, gently pinching and twisting it until she moaned into his mouth. Her other breast tingled, wanting the same attention.

Alex lifted her until she wrapped her legs around his waist and he walked them into deeper water. Pressing her back against the wall near the waterfall, he bent his head and took her other nipple in his mouth, sucking and licking the tip until she cried out for more. His sensual assault on her breasts was sending a zinging pleasure straight to her pussy, making her inner walls clench in response. She ached for his cock, was ready to beg for it.

His teeth grazed her overly sensitive nipple at the same time his fingers pinched her other one and she came, fisting her hands in his hair. While her pussy was still clenching and unclenching, he slid his cock inside of her nice and slow. The feeling of him stretching her, filling her, was enough to trigger a second orgasm. He eased out and surged back in, burying himself to the hilt. As he began pistoning in and out of her, she held on for the ride of her life. Every thrust of his cock pushed her closer and closer to orgasm.

Bailey kissed him, her tongue seeking his. Her legs tightened around his waist as her body strained, reaching toward release. With one arm wrapped around her, Alex slid his hand down her body, plunging his fingers between the lips of her pussy. He rubbed her clit in small tight circles, making stars burst behind her eyelids. She came, calling his name, clinging to him as if her life depended on it. As her body began to relax, she felt him thrust into her one last time, spilling himself inside of her.

Alex kissed her temple. "We should go swimming more often."

She laughed and hugged him tight.

"I think we should get dressed and eat before dinner gets cold," he said, nuzzling her neck.

"Probably a good idea. But we definitely have to come out and do this again sometime."

He grinned. "Promise. We can even make it a weekly thing if you want."

"I wouldn't mind trying the lounge chairs next time."

"Don't forget the whirlpool tub inside big enough for two. We can always do that again."

"Oohh. I know what I want to do after dinner."

Alex kissed her. "We can do whatever you want, as long as you're in bed by my side at the end of the day."

She felt all warm and fuzzy and wished her heart wasn't involved. She was afraid it was going to get broken.

Chapter Six

Later that night, Bailey stared at the bed uncertainly. She'd dressed in her pajamas, and while she was tired, she was also a little uneasy. It wasn't that she hadn't spent the night with a guy before. There had been men who'd stayed all night, even if Alex hadn't been one of them. But this was different.

Judging by the spare change, pen and paperback on the nightstand to the left of the bed, that was the side Alex slept on. She moved around to the opposite side and pulled down the covers. She slipped between the sheets and pulled the covers up to her chest. The bed was comfortable, the pillow soft, but she still felt ill at ease. She fidgeted and turned over onto her side, facing the window. With a sigh, she closed her eyes and focused on falling asleep.

Bailey did her best to clear her mind, but thoughts of Alex kept popping up. They'd made love again after dinner, and she knew that was exactly what it was for her. While he'd mentioned making love to her before, she felt that, to Alex, it was still just sex. If anything, he'd probably used the phrase to make her feel better about their odd relationship. That bothered her a great deal, but she knew she would just have to get used to it. He might be faithful to her, but he never said anything about falling in love with her.

She wondered what their lives would be like a few months from now when she was growing large with their child. Would their relationship still be the same as it was today? Or would it evolve into something more? Would he still want her with the same intensity when she was fat as a cow? She'd seen pregnant women who were beautiful, but she wasn't certain that she would be one of them.

Her thoughts were still in a whirlwind when she heard Alex step into the room and close the door. Trying not to tense, she concentrated on keeping her breathing nice and even. She listened to him undress and felt the bed dip as he slid under the covers. A moment later, his arm snaked around her waist and pulled her tight against his chest. He kissed the side of her neck.

"Good night," he whispered in her ear.

"Good night," she murmured.

He tightened his arm around her, snuggling her closer. She forced herself to relax. This was just Alex after all. They'd been intimate countless times, and yet, sleeping in his arms felt like the most intimate thing they'd done so far. She had to admit that she liked feeling his strength surround her, having his scent envelop her. She felt cared for, almost loved. But she knew that was ridiculous because there was no way that he loved her.

She knew where he worked, that he loved his motorcycle, even if he did say he was selling it, and she'd learned a little about his family and his misspent youth. During their time packing and over dinner, she'd learned a lot about him, but she still felt as if they were strangers. So how could she feel so strongly about someone she barely knew? Her heart raced every time she saw him, his voice made her want to melt, and his touch... Lord but his touch set her on fire unlike anyone ever had before! Even after all the times they'd made love throughout the afternoon, she still wanted him.

They hadn't talked much about her past, not since their dinner the other night. She knew that opening up about the things that caused her the most pain had changed something between them, but she wasn't sure what. Alex had seemed different ever since that talk. Did he pity her? She didn't need anyone's pity. She may have been weak when she'd first lost Josh, but she was strong now. While she'd been through a lot, she'd still managed to make something of her life, and she was damn proud of that fact.

Just thinking about Josh made her heart ache. She would always miss him, but she hoped that maybe Alex would be the one to help dull the pain even more. No one would ever replace Josh, but she had enough room in her heart for both of them. Assuming Alex wanted a place in her heart at some point in the future.

With her chaotic thoughts swirling through her mind, she finally dropped off to sleep, her dreams filled with what the future might hold for her and her unborn child.

* * *

In the morning, she stretched and rolled over, facing an empty bed. There was a note on Alex's pillow letting her know that he'd gone to pick up the truck and meet the guys at her apartment. It seemed that he expected her to stay put while he finished the move. Since her car was still at the apartment, she had no choice but to comply, but that didn't mean she had to like it.

While Alex was gone, she busied herself dusting, mopping and vacuuming her new home. She polished every wooden surface until they gleamed and cleaned every window until they shone brightly. When she was finished, she was exhausted but in a good way. Taking her tired slightly aching body out back, she stretched out in a lounge chair by the pool and closed her eyes. It was warm outside, but the sun felt nice on her skin. Being in the pool would have felt better, but she didn't have her suit and wasn't about to go skinny dipping on the off chance Alex brought company home with him. She soaked up the rays, enjoying the peace and quiet. Before long, she drifted off to sleep.

It was an hour later that Alex found her snoozing in the chair. She felt his warm calloused hand stroke down her arm and blinked her eyes open. Looking up at him, she smiled sleepily.

"You're back."

"Yes, I am. And I see you've been busy. I don't think the house has been this clean since I moved in."

"I didn't get to the bathrooms or kitchen. And the wood floors need to be waxed."

"No wax. It might make you slip and fall."

"Fine. No wax."

He grinned. "I do believe you're already nesting. One of the articles I read said you would go through that phase."

She sat up. "I take it all of my stuff is moved?"

He nodded. "And your car is in the garage. I had one of the guys drive it over for you."

"Thanks. It will be nice not to be housebound tomorrow. Not that I had a particular place I wanted to go today, but it would have been nice to know I had the option to leave."

"We still need to discuss your car. An SUV would be much better for you."

"I'm not letting you dictate every aspect of my life! You're already trying to tell me what to eat and drink, what to wear, where to live... where does it end? Next you'll want me to remove the streaks in my hair."

He eyed the purple streaks in question, but didn't say anything.

"If I decide to trade my car in on something different, it will be my decision and mine alone. Is that clear?"

He narrowed his eyes. "You're not going to fit a car seat in the back of that Bug."

"It isn't like I have to put one in there right now. I'm only a few weeks along, which means I have nine months to decide."

With a shake of his head, Alex backed down. Bailey smiled, thrilled with her victory. She knew it wouldn't last forever, but at least she'd silenced him for the time being. Eyeing the pool with longing, she glanced up at Alex.

"You didn't bring friends back with you, did you?"

"They're unloading the truck. Why?"

She sighed. "I was hoping to go for a swim, but I still don't have my bathing suit."

"You definitely aren't swimming until they're gone."

"How much longer will they be here?"

"Maybe fifteen minutes, twenty tops. Think you can hang on that long?"

She nodded. "I think I'll just rest here until they're gone, if that's okay."

"That's fine. You can meet them later."

She watched Alex walked back into the house and closed her eyes again.

Chapter Seven

It had been several days since Bailey had moved in with Alex and they'd settled into a routine. While he was gone during the day, she worked in the home office. In the early afternoon, she'd take a break and swim a few laps in the pool to cool off and relax, then she'd have lunch before returning to work for another hour or two. She'd managed to have dinner ready for Alex almost every night when he got home, but tonight she just wasn't feeling well. She'd been queasy ever since she woke up, had thrown up several times, and nothing she did made it go away.

She'd stretched out in bed an hour ago and now she was curled in on herself, cradling her belly. A glance at the clock told her Alex would be home soon and she wanted to be out of bed to greet him, but something told her that wasn't going to happen. She'd never been so miserable in her life. Was this just part of pregnancy, or was it something more?

A door slammed downstairs startling her. It was too soon for Alex to be home, but she didn't know of anyone else who had a key. She tried to get out of bed when her belly spasmed and wave of nausea hit her hard. Curling up, she closed her eyes and prayed for it to end.

Heavy footsteps sounded down the hall and stopped in the bedroom doorway. "Bailey?"

The footsteps approached and Alex kneeled beside the bed. He brushed the hair out of her eyes and caressed her cheek. "What's wrong?" he asked.

"I don't know. I've been sick all day."

"You're pale and clammy. Why didn't you go to the doctor?"

"I can't move. I barely made it down the hall to the office this morning, and I wasn't able to stay for very long. Alex, what's wrong with me?"

He gently scooped her up in his arms. "I don't know, but we're going to find out."

Marching downstairs with her, he entered the garage and settled her in the passenger seat of the Mustang. After he'd buckled her in, he closed the door and hurried around the car. He slid in and closed the door, starting the car almost simultaneously and backed down the driveway. In less than fifteen minutes, he was pulling into the minor medical parking lot.

Alex lifted her into his arms and carried her inside. He settled her on a chair before approaching the front window. She couldn't hear what he was saying, but a moment later he carried a clipboard over with paperwork attached.

"I know you don't feel well, but I'm going to need your help with this paperwork. The sooner we complete it, the sooner the doctor can see you."

She made a feeble attempt at grasping the clipboard, but it slipped through her fingers. Instead, she opted for telling Alex the information and letting him fill out the forms. It took a little longer that way, but eventually they finished and he took the clipboard back to the window.

When he returned, he gently took her hand. "They said it shouldn't be too long."

She leaned into him, resting her head on his shoulder, drawing from his strength. She felt weak as a kitten and the longer she was out of bed, the worse it became. Bailey honestly wasn't sure if she could stand up and walk if the need arose. If Alex weren't with her, she didn't know what she would do.

Before long, they called her name. Alex lifted her into his arms and carried her into the back. The doctor looked concerned and motioned to the paper covered table. "Put her up there."

Alex set her down gently, but he didn't move very far away.

"So what seems to be the trouble?" the older man asked as he closed the door.

"When I got home, I found her curled up in bed. She was pale and clammy, and she was gripping her stomach."

"Any other symptoms, young lady?"

"I threw up several times and I've been nauseated all day."

"Hmm."

"She's pregnant," Alex said. "Only a few weeks along."

"Well, while that could certainly account for the nausea, the rest sounds like a bug to me. There's a nasty virus going around. You'll need to be extra careful and make sure you stay hydrated. We've already lost three people to this virus in the past two weeks."

Bailey paled even further. "I've tried drinking water all day, but I had a hard time keeping it down."

"Try Gatorade. If you can't keep that down, or any other liquids, we'll have to admit you to the hospital and hook you up to an IV. It's important for anyone to stay hydrated, but you more than most since you're expecting."

"I'll try."

"She'll do more than try. We'll stop by the store on the way home so she can pick out any flavor of Gatorade she wants," Alex said.

Bailey glanced up at him, but didn't say anything. While she hated that he was dictating to her again, she liked the fact that he wanted to take care of her. It had been a long time since someone of the opposite sex had seen to her needs.

The doctor filled out a form and handed it to Alex. "Just give this to the ladies up front and pay for your visit, then you can be on your way. If there's any change, if she should get any worse, I want to see her again, or take her straight to the emergency room. Don't take any chances with her."

Alex nodded and took the form. Somehow, he managed to hold onto the paper and lift Bailey into his arms again. When he reached the front of the office, he set her down and handed the form to the ladies behind the counter. When they told him how much the visit cost, he handed them a credit card.

Bailey hated that Alex was paying for her visit. If she'd thought of it, she would have grabbed her purse. She'd find out how much it was and pay him back. It was only fair. With a groan, she gripped her stomach and decided to focus on something else. Like breathing without wanting to vomit.

She saw Alex stuff his wallet into his back pocket and then he turned to face her. He gave her a gentle smile before picking her up. He took her to the car and made good on his word to the doctor, taking her to the grocery store before heading home.

It felt like hours before she was lounging in bed again, the covers tucked around her, a bottle of Gatorade on the bedside table. Alex had smoothed her hair back from her face, kissed the top of her head and left her to rest, with a promise to check on her shortly. She'd closed her eyes and dozed a bit, trying to sip on her drink every half hour. But two hours later found her hunched over the toilet wishing she were dead.

Alex eased into the room behind her and held her hair back. "How long have you been in here?"

"A few minutes," she mumbled. "The Gatorade apparently didn't settle my stomach very well."

He wet a rag and wiped her face and mouth. "Do you feel well enough to go lie down again?"

She nodded weakly.

Alex carried her back to bed and tucked her in. "I know it's early, but if you think the TV won't bother you, I think I'll go ahead and come to bed. I don't like leaving you alone up here."

"That's fine," she murmured. "But I don't want to get you sick."

"Let me worry about that. Right now, my concern is you."

Bailey rolled onto her side and tucked her hand under her chin. Closing her eyes, she sighed.

Having Alex nearby would be nice, but she really did worry about giving whatever bug she'd caught.

When he entered the room again, she opened her eyes and watched as he stripped down to his boxers and climbed into bed. Hooking one arm around her, he pulled her close until her head rested on his shoulder.

Closing her eyes, Bailey relaxed into him. If Alex wasn't concerned about getting sick, then she wouldn't worry about it either. Besides, it felt far too good to be held.

Chapter Eight

The next morning, Alex woke to find Bailey splayed across him. She was soaked in sweat and looked completely washed out. He was more than just a little worried. Despite what the doctor had said yesterday, he would feel better if she were to be seen by the hospital. He didn't want to take any chances with her or their unborn child.

He didn't know when it had happened, but Bailey was starting to mean something to him, more than just the mother of his child. He didn't know how to label his feelings, and he wasn't sure he was even ready for that step yet. But he knew that he did care for her.

Easing out from under her, he went to the bathroom to get a cool damp cloth to wipe her down. Once he'd cleaned her up a bit, he changed her clothes. The fact that she didn't wake during the entire process worried him. She lay completely limp, unaware of anything going on around her.

Coming to a decision, he threw on some clothes and gathered her up in his arms. He was taking her to the hospital even if they sent them back home, just as long as someone looked at her and made sure she was okay. After hearing about the deaths the virus had caused, he wasn't taking any chances.

He broke every speed limit between his house and the ER parking lot, and he was thankful to see the waiting room was nearly empty when he carried Bailey inside. The triage nurse called for a gurney so Alex could lay Bailey down, and as they wheeled her into the back, he began filling out paperwork. Once he was finished, he insisted on joining her.

A nurse led him to a small curtained off room and he sat beside Bailey, taking her hand in his. It looked so tiny and pale lying in his large palm, and he worried that she might not be strong enough to fight the virus that was attacking her. He willed her to open her eyes, but she lay still and lifeless, the rise and fall of her chest the only indication that she lived. He couldn't remember a time he'd been more scared.

It seemed like it took forever before a doctor came by, and Alex wasn't sure he liked the man. Doctor Owens looked like he was thirty, if that, making him a good six years younger than Alex, and he wondered just how much experience the man had. He didn't feel comfortable giving Bailey over to him but knew there wasn't much choice.

"How long has she been like this?" Doctor Owens asked.

"I came home from work yesterday and discovered that she'd been sick all day. The med emergency doctor told us she had a virus. Then, this morning, I couldn't get her to wake up."

The doctor nodded. Pulling his stethoscope from around his neck, he listened to her heart and her stomach.

"She's pregnant," Alex said.

"Well, I don't like the fact that we can't wake her. How much did she have to drink yesterday?"

"Not much. Every time she drank a little, it would come back up."

The doctor nodded again, while feeling of her abdomen. "All right, I'm going to start her admit papers. Why don't you stay here and hold her hand, just let her know she isn't alone. A nurse will be by as soon as possible to move her to a room."

"You're keeping her?" Alex clarified.

"Yes. I think she should stay for at least a day or two. Maybe longer, depending on how she reacts to the IV we're going to give her. If all goes well, she'll be awake by dinnertime." The doctor paused. "I don't think I need to tell you just how serious this is. This virus is deadly. If you hadn't brought her in this morning, we may have lost her. And honestly, there's still no guarantee that she'll pull through."

Alex paled. "Thank you, doctor."

Alex took Bailey's hand in his again and rubbed his thumb over her knuckles. He was glad he'd brought her, glad he'd trusted his instincts. He didn't know what he would do if he lost her now.

Now that he was faced with the possibility of losing her, he had to be honest with himself. He knew he cared for her, had known for quite some time, but was it something more? Was it possible that Mr. Love 'em and Leave 'em had real feelings for someone? He'd known from their first encounter that there was something special about Bailey, that she was different from any woman he'd ever known before. The moment he'd looked into her eyes, he'd known that just one night would never be enough. Of course, it didn't hurt that the sex was explosive. No one made him feel the way Bailey did. Just seeing her was enough to make him want her.

Could he possibly love her? Alex had never been in love before so he wasn't sure what it felt like. The fact that he didn't want another woman was a big clue. The only woman he wanted in his bed, in his life, was Bailey. The baby had sped up the process, but he was certain that they would have ended up together eventually. The thought of losing her hit him like a thousand knives. He realized his life wouldn't be complete without her. And while he'd never told her, he'd gotten used to the idea of being a daddy. The thought of a baby with her pretty blonde hair made him smile.

She had to make it through this. If she pulled through, he'd tell her how he felt, he'd make sure she knew how important she was to him. He lifted her hand and kissed her palm.

A nurse opened the curtain and smiled at him. "We have a room ready for her, if you'll follow me."

Alex stood and followed behind the nurse. They went down several halls, up the elevator to the third floor and down another series of hallways. He wasn't sure he'd make it back to the main door if his life depended on it. Finally, they made it to Bailey's assigned room. Two male nurses came in and helped transfer her to the bed. After everyone left, Alex resumed his vigil at her bedside.

When dinner came and went and Bailey still didn't wake, he thought his heart would stop. Since she hadn't woken, did that mean she wasn't going to make it? Was she going to die?

No, Alex refused to believe that he was going to lose her after just finding her. He wouldn't let her go. Ever.

Chapter Nine

Alex's friend, Parker, had called a short while ago and Alex had told him what was going on with Bailey. And now, his friend stood just inside the hospital room door. Alex was glad to see him. It was nice to know that he had people who cared about him and would be there for him when things got rough.

"How is she?" his friend asked.

"The same. The doctors aren't saying anything, and that worries me. The first doctor said she could wake up as soon as dinner, but she hasn't moved. What if she doesn't make it?" he asked, voicing his concerns.

"You can't think that way. You have to stay positive."

Alex nodded. "I'm trying."

Parker noticed Alex's hands, twisting and braiding a piece of ribbon he'd acquired from the florist shop on the main level of the hospital. It was all he could think of at the moment, and he wanted to have something to give Bailey, something to show her what she meant to him.

"If you don't think she's going to make it, why are you twisting that bit of ribbon into a ring?" Parker asked.

"Because I want her to pull through. I realized that I don't want to go on without her. Until today, I hadn't realized just how much she means to me."

"I told the guys. Everyone's pulling for her to make a full recovery."

"Thanks."

Parker glanced at Bailey one more time before looking at Alex. "I'll leave you two alone, but if you need anything, just call. You know I'm here no matter what."

Alex slapped Parker on the back. "That means a lot to me."

Parker turned and left, leaving him alone with Bailey once more.

Alex stood beside the bed and took her hand in his. Looking at the bit of ribbon in his hand, he eased it onto the ring finger of her left hand. It wasn't fancy, but it was all he had at the moment. He could replace it with something grand later, assuming Bailey said yes.

He'd flinched whenever the word marriage came up before, but now things were different. Now he realized that he wanted Bailey in his life forever. He didn't want to just live with her, he wanted to share his life with her on a deeper level. He only hoped she felt the same way.

Kissing her hand, he settled into his chair once more to sit and wait. That was all he could do, and it was killing him.

* * *

Several hours later, Bailey's eyes fluttered open. Alex smiled in relief and kissed her forehead.

"Where am I?" she croaked, her throat obviously dry.

"You're in the hospital. I brought you here this morning when you wouldn't wake up."

"What happened?"

"Do you remember yesterday?"

She frowned. "I wasn't feeling well."

"Honey, you were more than not feeling well. You scared the hell out of me."

"But I'm better now?"

"I'll have to get a nurse or doctor in here to tell us for sure, but I think the fact that you're awake is a good sign that you're on the mend."

She reached for his hand and looked at hers in confusion. "What's this?"

He cleared his throat. "I had hoped you wouldn't notice until you were feeling a bit better."

"That doesn't answer my question," she said, her voice gaining strength.

"It's an engagement ring, sort of. I know I should have asked before putting it on you, but I did a lot of thinking today. In the past, I've run from marriage, even the thought of it, but the idea of being married to you doesn't terrify me. It fills me with peace. I don't want us to just live together anymore, Bailey. I want you to be my wife."

Tears shimmered in her eyes. "Why?"

He looked taken aback. "Why?"

She nodded. "Why do you want me to be your wife?"

"I thought I just told you."

"Do you love me?" she asked.

"I... I care about you more than I've ever cared about anyone. I don't know what love feels like, but I guess it could be love."

"You guess?" she asked, sounding a bit down.

"I know that I don't want to spend another day of my life without you. When I thought I was going to lose you, it felt like my heart was being ripped out. All I could think about was that I never got a chance to tell you how I feel, to let you know how important you are to me."

Her eyes met his again. "Do you love me?" she asked again.

He took a steadying breath. "Yeah, I love you."

She smiled at him then. "I love you, too. I have since the first day I moved into your house. I was just too scared to tell you. I didn't know what you would think or how you would feel about it."

"I probably would have been terrified, honestly."

She nodded. Pressing a hand to her stomach, she asked, "The baby?"

"Seems to be fine."

Alex settled in the chair again and took her hand once more. The realization that he loved her made his heart pound, but knowing she loved him in return was the greatest gift he could have ever received. Well, that and their unborn child. They were going to be a family, really and truly this time.

He pushed the call button on the side of the bed and waited on a nurse to respond. When the desk asked if he needed assistance, he informed them that Bailey was awake. It was only a minute or so later that someone came to the room. After checking her vitals and asking her a series of questions, they were assured a doctor would be in to see them shortly.

Alex didn't care how long it took. Bailey was awake, and she was going to marry him. Nothing else mattered.

Chapter Ten

Three days later, they were home from the hospital and Bailey was almost back to her old self. She still had to take it easy because she tired rather quickly, but she was able to get up and move around. It was nice to be home and in her own bed again, and even nicer to be able to snuggle up next to Alex at night. He'd had to return to work, but she'd promised not to do anything that could be harmful to her health.

Sitting at her computer, she answered all of the emails she'd missed during her stint in the hospital. She explained her absence and looked over the projects she had due and new ones coming in. Deciding she felt well enough to work a little, she occupied herself with a book cover, something simple to get back into the swing of things. It took her longer than usual, and once she was done, she decided to move on to another project. By the time Alex got home, she'd finished two book covers and three bookmarks. Almost all of her work was caught up.

"What are you doing in here?" he asked, standing in the office doorway.

"Getting some work done."

He frowned. "Is that wise? Shouldn't you be resting?"

"I didn't do anything I couldn't handle. I promise I'm fine."

His gaze raked her from head to toe, taking in the skimpy tank top and short shorts. "How are you feeling?"

She saw the heat in his gaze and knew what he was asking. She wasn't sure which of them wanted the intimacy more, but was she ready yet? Maybe if they took things slowly… of course, things tended to be a bit wild whenever they were intimate.

"You're thinking awfully hard," he said.

"If you're gentle…"

She didn't get any more out before he scooped her into his arms and began striding toward the bedroom. He carefully laid her on the bed and began removing his clothes. Once he'd completely stripped, he began removing her clothes slowly, dropping them on the floor one at a time.

Covering her body with his, he sealed her lips with his. It had only been four days since they'd been intimate, but it felt like it had been weeks. She was starved for him, and she was certain he felt the same. His forearms braced the bulk of his weight, but everywhere they touched felt like it was on fire.

Alex trailed kisses down her neck to her breasts. Cupping her breast, he sucked her nipple into his mouth, grazing it with his teeth. She moaned and arched into him, wanting more. Releasing her breast, his hand moved down her body, dipping between her legs. She was already wet and ready for him. He slid a finger inside of her and back out, spreading her juices over her clit.

Using small circles, he teased the engorged nub. Bailey spread her legs wider, begging for more. Alex moved to the other nipple, teasing and tormenting it the same as the other while he continued to lightly caress her most sensitive place. She lifted her hips, wanting to feel his cock fill her. She'd never felt so empty.

Alex continued to take her higher and higher until she thought she couldn't take anymore. When she was near mindless from pleasure, he lightly pinched her clit, sending her over the edge. As her pussy spasmed in release, he eased his cock inside of her, filling her, stretching her, making her feel complete. Her orgasm hadn't completely stopped before he began moving, gliding in and out of her nice and easy, drawing it out.

Releasing her nipple, his lips returned to hers. She opened her mouth under his, welcoming the invasion of his tongue as he tasted her. His tongue mimicked his cock, plunging into her over and over. She gripped his shoulders as her body tensed, preparing itself. The next time he entered her, she let go, letting her orgasm crash over her. As her pussy convulsed around his cock, he began thrusting into her harder and faster, until he too found his release, spilling himself inside of her.

Afterward, they lay in one another's arms, spent. Bailey burrowed into Alex, wanting to be as close to him as possible, despite their sweat slicked skin. As she lay there, she realized she'd never told him something very important. They'd confessed their love for one another. He'd even gone to the store the other morning and purchased her the most exquisite engagement ring she'd ever seen. But she'd never really agreed to marry him. Something she planned on correcting now.

"Alex, my answer is yes."

"Pardon?"

"At the hospital you gave me a ring and said you wanted to marry me. I never said whether or not I would." She looked up at him. "The answer is yes."

He kissed her gently. "I promise you won't regret it. I can't promise that we'll never fight, but I promise to always love you, to make a happy home for you and our baby."

Tears gathered in Bailey's eyes. "That's all I could ask for. I love you, Alex."

"I love you, too."

She pulled his head down for a kiss, and with wandering hands, set about showing him just how much he meant to her.

About the Author

Jessica Coulter Smith has lived in various places around the US, from Georgia to California. She currently resides in Tennessee. An author of adult romance and YA romances (under Jessie Coler), she began her writing career as a poet. Her first poem was published when she was 16, but that was just the start. Many published poems later, along with an Editor's Choice Award for "My World is Tumbling Down", she is quickly making a name for herself as a novelist.

When she isn't writing, Jessica enjoys spending time with her family, reading, or going to the beach. She's also an avid horse lover and owns an American Saddlebred gelding, who occasionally needs to be reminded he's not a dog.

Jessica loves to hear from her fans! You may email her at JessicaCoulterSmith@yahoo.com or visit her at her website: http://www.jessicacoultersmith.com/.

Printed in Great Britain
by Amazon.co.uk, Ltd.,
Marston Gate.